OH NO
BUDDY!

Written by **JODY GRIGGS**

Illustrated by **ALISHA OBER**

ISBN 978-1-7363386-1-2 (hardcover)
ISBN 978-1-7363386-0-5 (paperback)

Gigglesome Publishing
Memphis, Tennessee

This Book Belongs to

_____

Brown and black, with a touch of white.

Afraid of his shadow, he barks at his fright.

He jumps after birds and runs after squirrels,

Chasing his tail into dizzying whirls.

He's a happy young pup, and his name is Buddy,
Runs through the house with paws that are muddy.

OH NO BUDDY!

Out in his backyard, he watches and patrols,

Barking at noises and digging some holes.

Sniffing those holes, he gets dirt on his nose,

Now he needs a bath; let's get out the hose.

He runs off and hides; now he just wants to pout.

That dog is into everything and makes you want to shout!

OH NO BUDDY!

Buddy's really not bad; he's actually quite smart.

A little curious, and that is always the start.

Hey, there's a pretty pillow that looks like some fun.

It's all over the house. Now look what you've done!

He thinks this is fun and barks, "Let's play."

I'm at my wits end and I simply want to say,

OH NO BUDDY!

In the mornings he is playful, and he wants to play fetch,

But with his game there are twists and a bit of a catch.

If there is mischief to get into, he is sure to find,

Remember those new shoes that are one of a kind?

Well, you better get the broom, as well as the mop,

Cause Buddy just turned them into his own lollipop.

OH NO BUDDY!

Something good is in the kitchen and
Buddy gives it a whiff.

His nose is in the air; he smells it . . .
sniff sniff.

He waits for the right time, when no
one is looking,

Because he thinks it's for him that you
have been cooking.

The food on the table; where did it go?
The mystery is solved, I think we all know.

OH No BUDDY!

Now in the dog park and what does he see?

Toys of all sizes and room to run, Whoopee!

There are balls of all colors and none are the same.

I wonder which one Buddy wants for his game.

Of all the toys to choose from, which one does he pick?

He runs past the toys and picks up a stick.

OH NO BUDDY!

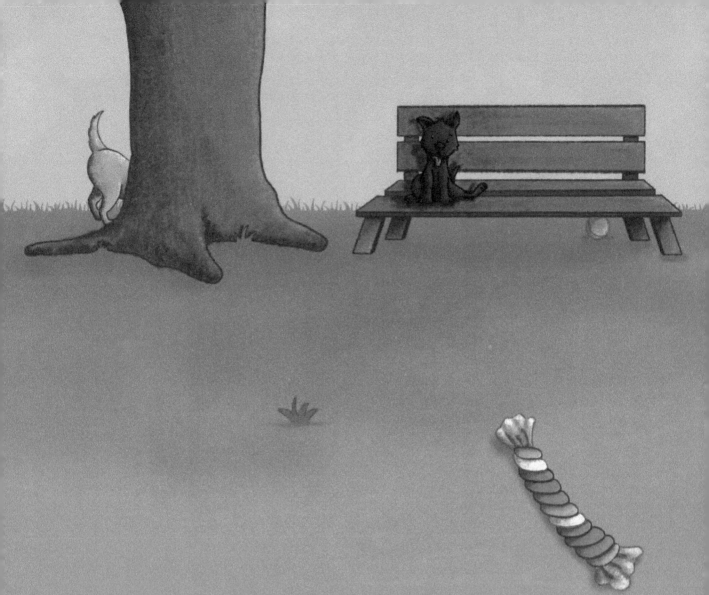

With the stick in his mouth, he prances about.

He is king of the dog park and there is no doubt.

Although there are dogs that are bigger in size,

None of them have the stick, the really great prize.

Buddy runs off and says, "I want to be fair,
But I love my old stick and don't wish to share."

OH NO BUDDY!

Buddy doesn't like a doghouse; he prefers to sleep in bed.

The only thing he likes more is getting treats and being fed.

Well, I guess there are two other things, like rubbing his belly,

As well as sneaking bites of biscuits and jelly.

Things have got to change with this dog, the situation isn't right.
He snores so loudly, I stayed up half the night!

OH NO BUDDY!

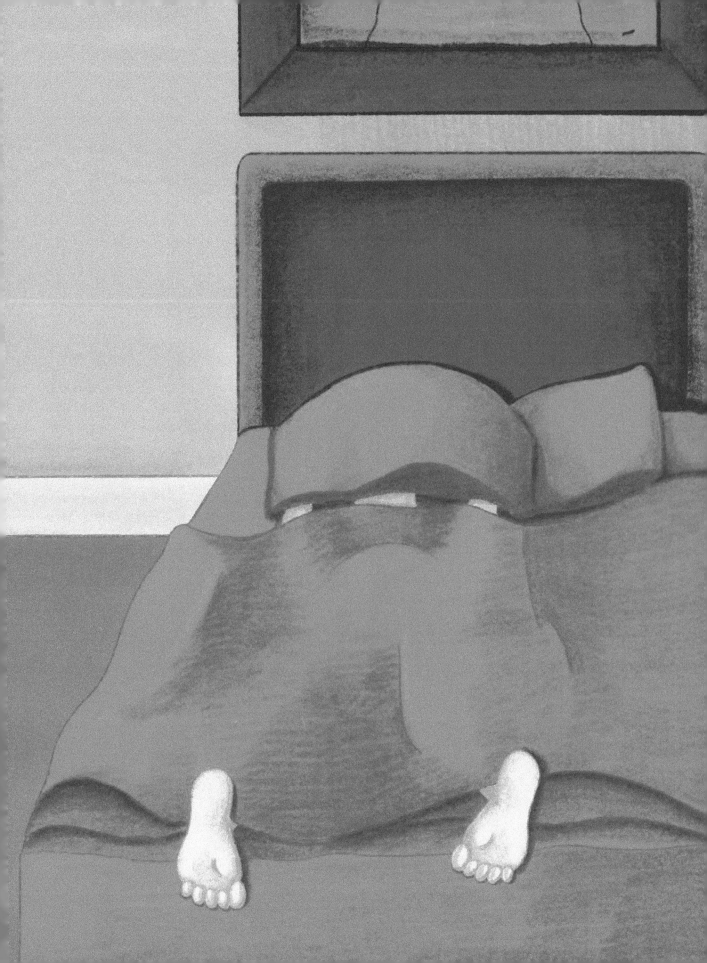

But when I come home after being out for a while,

He greets me with a tail wag and can actually smile.

As I reach down and rub behind his big, floppy ear,

I realize the joy he brings and all his good cheer.

He was a homeless little pup, some kind of a hound,
A real-life doggie version of the lost and found.

OH MY BUDDY!

THe END

ABOUT BUDDY:

Abandoned as a puppy, Buddy was taken in by a local animal rescue group. He arrived at our home a few weeks later. "Just let us bring him by your house to see how he likes it. No commitment," the volunteer with the rescue group told us. He never left.

This book is about the happiness, as well as the "throw your hands up the air" moments that he brings. Buddy truly is a real-life lost and found story.

Part of the proceeds from each book will fund a donation to the local Human Society in the hopes that more lost animals will find forever homes, just like Buddy.

CPSIA information can be obtained
at www.ICGtesting.com
Printed in the USA
BVHW020721291220
596588BV00010BA/20